D0917891

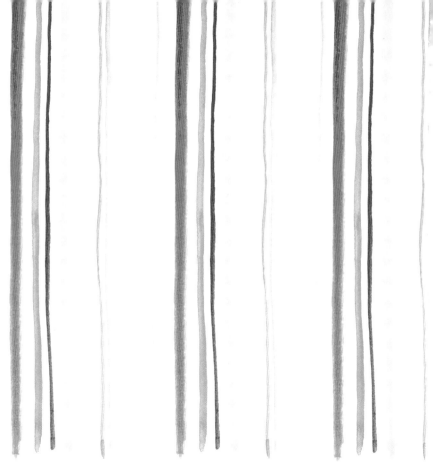

♥ let's be rudie nudies ♥ !

A naughty little book of love for you!

Juicylucy ♥

ℛℛ
RAVETTE PUBLISHING

First published in 2008 by
Ravette Publishing Ltd
PO Box 876, Horsham
West Sussex RH12 9GH
Reprinted 2008, 2009

© 2007 Juicy Lucy Designs
All rights reserved.

www.juicylucydesigns.com

This book is sold subject to the condition that it shall not,
by way of trade or otherwise, be lent, resold, hired out
or otherwise circulated without the publisher's prior consent
in any form of binding or cover other than that in which it is
published and without a similar condition including this condition
being imposed on the subsequent purchaser.

ISBN: 978-1-84161-299-7

Sometimes when I look at you..

..I start to dribble..

..I think I'm probably
going to show you..

my knickers. x

holding your hand,

is one of my favourite
things to do

(holding your willy is the other)

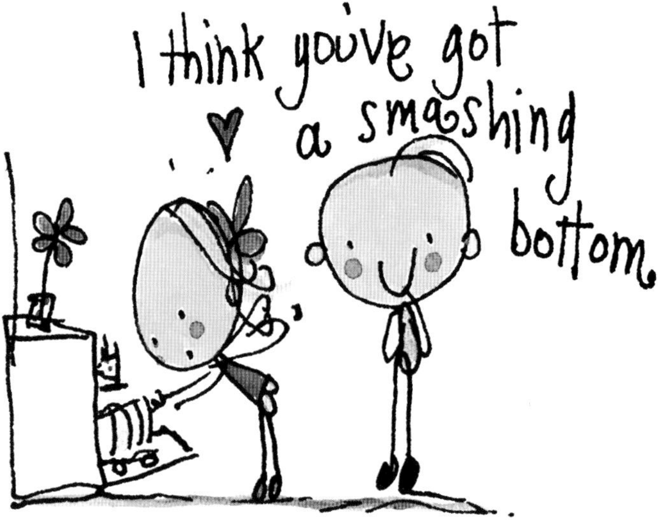
I think you've got a smashing bottom.

I particularly like you with your pants off.

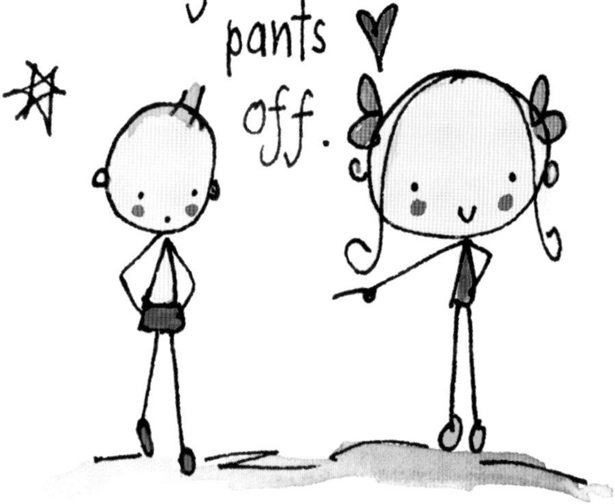

What I love about you,
is

Your willy.

being rude with you

.. is my favourite
thing to do ..

(well that and eating cake)

thinking of you makes my

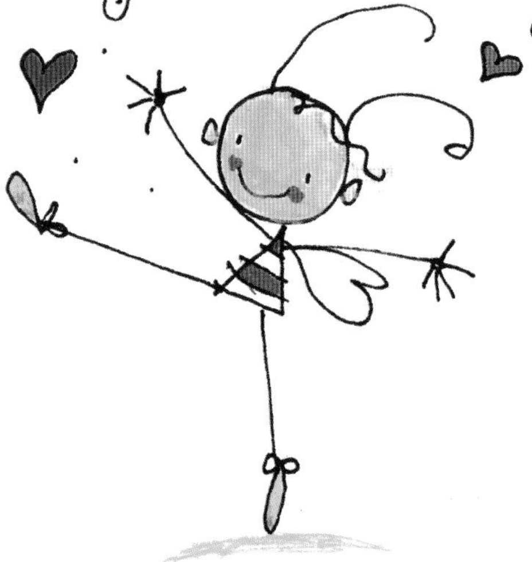

fanny feel funny.

nice
shlong.

I like it
when you
slip
me
one.

..You activate my love radar!..

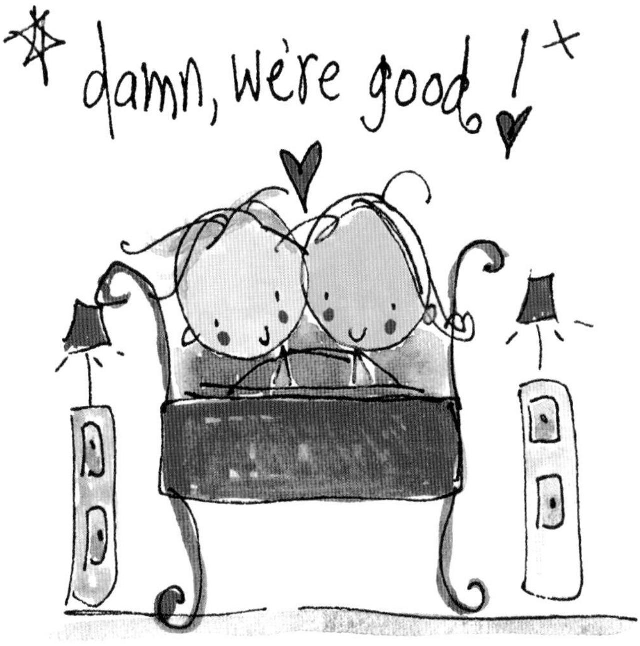
damn, we're good!

You've got the nicest

Willy I've ever seen ..x

oh come here,

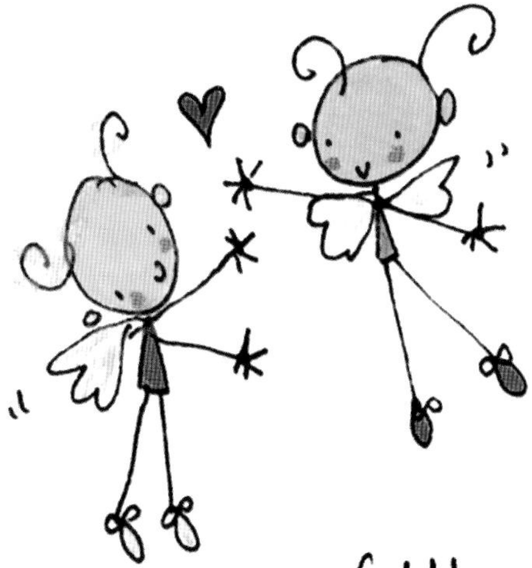

and let me fiddle with you.

you make me

too excited to sleep!

If you're good
I'll show you

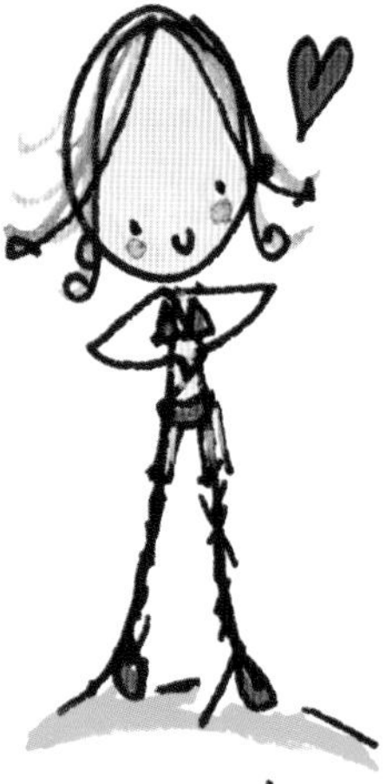

my front bottom.

quick, get your kit off!

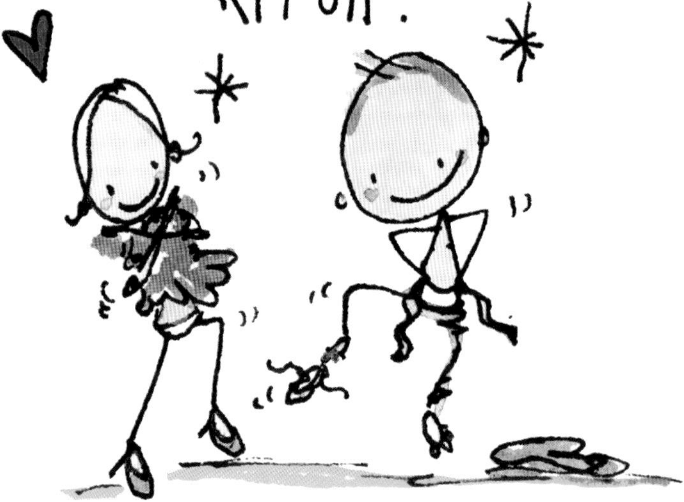

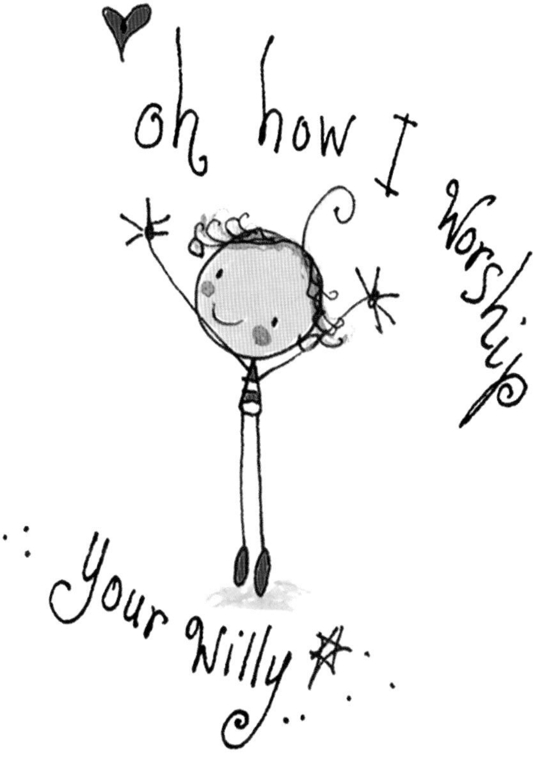
oh how I worship
your willy

nice
ass

You are, quite simply, the best shag I've ever had! x

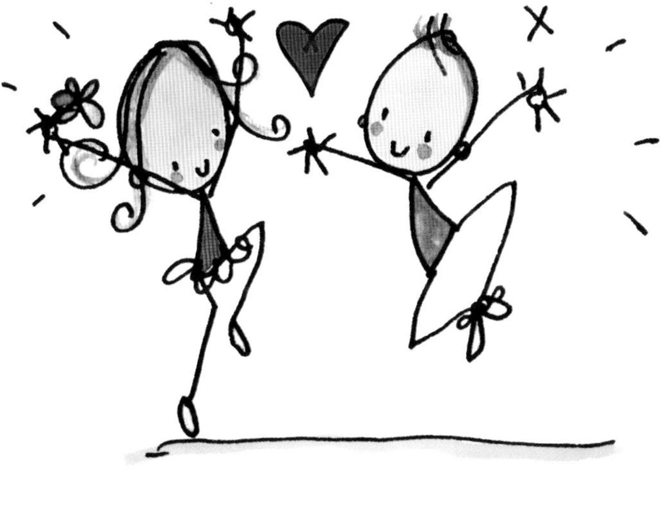

the reason I love you is..

..you're filthy..

.nice nipples.

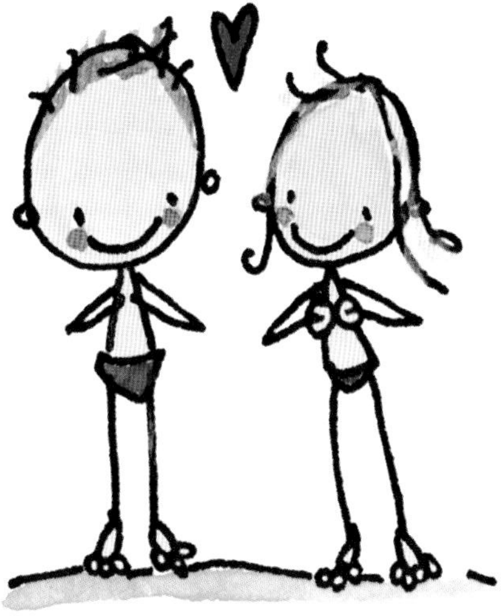

.. I love...

.. getting jiggy with you !

I like it when you

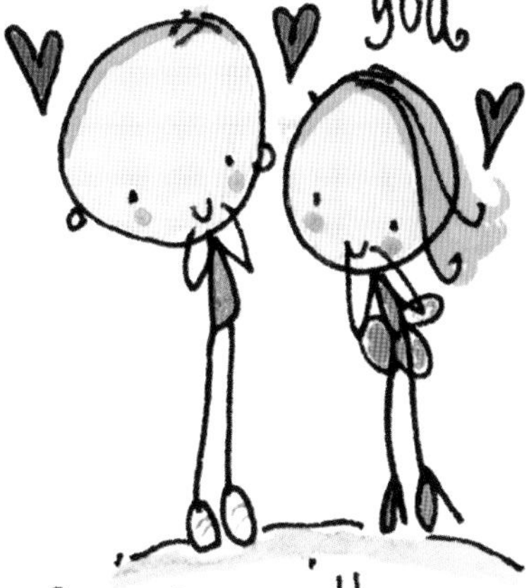

fiddle with my giblets.

This voucher entitles the bearer to a big fat juicy shag

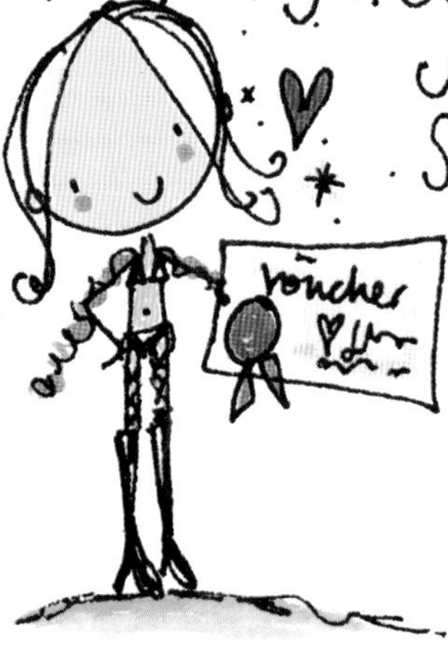